In the Forests
of the Night

This Large Print Book carries the
Seal of Approval of N.A.V.H.

In the Forests of the Night

Amelia Atwater-Rhodes

Thorndike Press • Waterville, Maine

Published in 2002 by arrangement with Random House Children's Books, a division of Random House, Inc.

Thorndike Press Large Print Young Adult Series.

The tree indicium is a trademark of Thorndike Press.

The text of this Large Print edition is unabridged.
Other aspects of the book may vary from the original edition.

Set in 16 pt. Plantin by Elena Picard.

Printed in the United States on permanent paper.

Library of Congress Cataloging-in-Publication Data

Atwater-Rhodes, Amelia.
    In the forests of the night / Amelia Atwater-Rhodes.
        p. cm.
    Summary: Risika, a teenage vampire, wanders back in time to the year 1684 when, as a human, she died and was transformed against her will.
    ISBN 0-7862-4761-4 (lg. print : hc : alk. paper)
    1. Large type books. [1. Vampires — Fiction. 2. Witches — Fiction. 3. Time travel — Fiction. 4. Youths' writings. 5. Large type books.] I. Title.
    PZ7.A8925 In 2002
    [Fic]—dc21   2002028726

IN THE FORESTS OF THE NIGHT *is dedicated to everyone who contributed to the story, especially:*

Julie Nann for her excellent teaching skills. Carolyn Barnes for talking to my agent about me. All the members of the Candle Light circle for their slightly insane inspiration. Sarita Spillert for her encouragement. Dan Hogan for enduring a telephone conversation at four in the morning. Laura Bombrun for her house, which coincidentally is exactly the same as Risika's. Also, I need to mention my family: my heroic father, William; my brilliant and inspiring sister, Rachel; my beautiful and slightly telepathic mother, Susan; and my overly insightful cousin, Nathan. I love you all.

The Tiger

Tiger! Tiger! Burning bright
In the forests of the night,
What immortal hand or eye
Could frame thy fearful symmetry?

In what distant deeps or skies
Burnt the fire of thine eyes?
On what wings dare he aspire?
What the hand dare seize the fire?

And what shoulder, and what art,
Could twist the sinews of thy heart?
And when thy heart began to beat,
What dread hand? and what dread feet?

What the hammer? what the chain?
In what furnace was thy brain?
What the anvil? what dread grasp?
Dare its deadly terrors clasp?

When the stars threw down their spears,
And watered heaven with their tears,
Did He smile His work to see?
Did He who made the Lamb, make thee?

Tiger! Tiger! Burning bright
In the forests of the night,
What immortal hand or eye,
Dare frame thy fearful symmetry?

William Blake

PROLOGUE

NOW

A cage of steel.

It is a cruel thing to do, to cage such a beautiful, passionate animal as if it was only a dumb beast, but humans do so all too often. They even cage themselves, though their bars are made of society, not of steel.

The Bengal tiger is gold with black stripes through its fur, and it is the largest of the felines. The sign reads *"Panthera tigris tigris";* it is simply a fancy name for *tiger.* I call this one Tora — she is my favorite animal in this zoo.

Tora walks toward me as I approach her cage. The minds of animals are different from the minds of humans, but I have spent much time with Tora, and we know each other very well. Though the thoughts of animals can rarely be translated into human thought, I understand her, and she understands me.

Such a beautiful animal should not be caged.

CHAPTER 1

NOW

I relinquish my human form for that of a hawk as I leave the zoo, which has been closed for hours. The security guard fell asleep rather suddenly, as many do upon meeting my eyes, so there is no one to witness my departure.

I could bring myself to my home instantly with my mind, but I enjoy the sensation of flying. Of all the animals, the birds are perhaps the most free, as they are able to move through the air and there is so little that can stop their flight.

I land only once, to feed, and then arrive back at my house in Massachusetts close to sunrise.

As I return to human form, I catch a glimpse of my hazy reflection in my bedroom mirror. My hair is long and is the color of old gold. My eyes, like those of all my kind, became black when I died. My skin is icy pale, and in the reflection it looks like mist. Today I wear black jeans and a black T-shirt. I do not always wear black, but that was the color of my mood today.

I do not care for the new, quickly built towns humans are so fond of scraping up out of plaster and paint, so I live in Concord, Massachusetts, a town with history. Concord has an aura — one that says "This land is ours, and we will fight to keep it that way." The people who live here keep Concord as it was long ago, though cars have replaced the horse-drawn carriages.

I live alone in one of Concord's original houses. Over the years I have made myself the long-lost daughter of several wealthy, elderly couples. That is how I "inherited" the home I live in.

Though I have no living relations that I know of, it is not difficult to influence the thoughts — and paperwork — of the human world. When mortals do begin to question me too closely, I can easily move to another location. However, I make no human friends no matter how long I stay in an area, so my existence and disappearance are rarely noticed.

12

My home is near the center of Concord; the view from the front windows is the Unitarian church, and the view from the back windows is a graveyard. Neither bothers me at all. Of course there are ghosts, but they do no harm besides the occasional startle or chill. They are usually too faint to be seen in daylight.

My home has no coffin in it; I sleep in a bed, thank you. I do have blackout curtains, but only because I usually find myself sleeping during the day. I do not burn in sunlight, but bright noonday sun does hurt my eyes.

The vampire myths are so confused that it is easy to see they were created by mortals. Some myths are true: my reflection is faint, and older ones in my line have no reflection at all. As for the other myths, there is little truth and many lies.

I do dislike the smell of garlic, but if your sense of smell was twenty times stronger than that of the average bloodhound, would you not dislike it as well? Holy water and crosses do not bother me — indeed, I have been to Christian services since I died, though I no longer look for solace in religion. I wear a silver ring set with a garnet stone, and the silver does not burn me. If someone hammered a stake through my heart I suppose I would die, but I do not play with humans, stakes, or mallets.

Since I am speaking about my kind, I might as well say something about myself. I was born to the name of Rachel Weatere in the year 1684, more than three hundred years ago.

The one who changed me named me Risika, and Risika I became, though I never asked what it meant. I continue to call myself Risika, even though I was transformed into what I am against my will.

My mind wanders back the road to my past, looking for a time when Rachel was still alive and Risika was not yet born.

CHAPTER 2

1701

There was ash on my pale skin from helping to put out the fire. As my sister, Lynette, had been preparing the evening meal, flames had leapt from the hearth like arms reaching out to grab her. My twin brother, Alexander, had been standing across the room from the hearth. He was convinced this accident was his fault.

"Am I damned?" he asked, staring past me at the now cold hearth.

How did he want me to answer? I was only seventeen, a girl still, and certainly not a cleric. I knew nothing of damnation and salvation that my twin brother did not know as well. Yet Alexander was looking at me, his golden eyes heavy with worry and shame, as if I should know everything.

"You should ask these things of a preacher, not me," I answered.

"Tell a preacher what I see? Tell him that I can look into people's minds, and that I can . . ."

He trailed off, but we both knew what the rest of the sentence was. For months Alexander had been trying to hide his powers, which were just as undesired as the fire had been. Shaking with fear, he had told me everything. He could sometimes hear the thoughts of those around him, though he tried to block them out. If he concentrated on an object, he would make it move. And, he had added, if he stared into a fire, he could make it rise or fall. Despite his efforts to control these powers, they were sometimes stronger than he was.

Lynette had been cooking supper. Now she was at the doctor's with our papa, being treated for burns.

"It is witchcraft," Alexander whispered, as if afraid to say the words any more loudly. "How can I tell a clergyman that?"

Once again I could not answer him. Alexander believed far more than I in the peril of the soul. Though we both said our prayers and went to church without fail, where I was skeptical, he was faithful. In truth, I was more afraid of the cold, commanding preachers than of the fires of Hell

16

they threatened us with. If I had the powers my brother was discovering, I would fear the church even more.

"Maybe that is what happened to our mother," Alexander said quietly. "Maybe I hurt her."

"Alexander!" I gasped, horrified that my brother could think such a thing. "How can you blame yourself for Mother's death? We were babies!"

"If I could lose control and hurt Lynette when I am seventeen, how much easier would it have been for me to lose control as a child?"

I did not remember my mother, though Papa sometimes spoke about her; she had died only a few days after Alexander and I were born. Her hair had been even fairer than my brother's and mine, but our eyes were exactly the same color as hers had been. An exotic honey gold, our eyes were dangerous in their uniqueness. Had my family not been so well accepted in the community, our eyes might have singled us out for accusations of witchcraft.

"You are not even certain *Lynette's* injuries are your fault," I told Alexander. Lynette was my papa's third child, born to his second wife; her mother had died only a year before of smallpox. "She was leaning too close to the fire, or maybe there was oil on the wood somehow. Even if you did cause it, it was not your fault."

"Witchcraft, Rachel," Alexander said softly. "How large a crime is that? I hurt someone, and I will not even go to the church to confess."

"It was not your fault!" Why did he insist on blaming himself for something he could not have prevented?

I saw my brother as a saint — he could hardly stand to watch Papa slaughter chickens for supper. I knew, even more surely than he did, that he could never intentionally hurt someone. "You never asked for these powers, Alexander," I told him quietly. "You never signed the Devil's book. You are trying to be forgiven for doing nothing wrong."

Papa returned home with Lynette late that evening. Her arms had been bandaged, but the doctor had said there would be no permanent damage. Alexander's guilt was still so strong — he made sure she rested, not using her hands, even though he had to do most of her work. As he and I cooked supper, he would occasionally catch my gaze, the question in his eyes pleading: *Am I damned?*

CHAPTER 3

NOW

Why am I thinking these things?

I find myself staring at the rose on my bed, so like one I was given nearly three hundred years ago. The aura around it is like a fingerprint: I can feel the strength and recognize the one who left it. I know him very well.

I have lived in this world for three hundred years, and yet I have broken one of its most basic rules. When I stopped last night to hunt after visiting Tora, I strayed into the territory of another.

My prey was clearly lost. Though not native to New York City, she had thought she knew where she was going.

The city at night is like a jungle. In the red glow of the unsleeping city the streets and alleys change and twist like shadows,

19

just like all the human — and not so human — predators that inhabit it.

As the sun set, my prey had found herself alone in a dark area of town. The streetlights were broken, and there were more shadows than light. She was afraid. Lost. Alone. Weak. Easy prey.

She turned onto another street, searching for something familiar. This street was darker than the one before, but not in a way a human would recognize. It was one of the many streets in America that belong to my kind. These streets look almost normal, less dangerous, though perhaps a bit more deserted. Illusions can be so comforting. My prey was walking into a Venus flytrap. If I did not, someone was going to kill her as soon as she entered one of the bars or set foot in a café, which had probably never served anything she would wish to drink.

She seemed to relax slightly when she saw the Café Sangra. None of the windows was broken, no one was collapsed against the building, and the place was open. She started toward the café, and I followed silently.

I sensed another human presence to my left and reached out with my mind to determine whether it was a threat. Walls went up in an instant. But they were weak, and I could tear through them if I tried. The human in question would feel it, though that did not matter to me.

"This isn't your land," he told me. Though I could sense a bit of a vampiric aura around him, he was definitely human. He was blood bonded to a vampire and probably even working for one, but not one of my kind. He was not a threat, so I did not even bother looking into his mind.

"This isn't your land," he told me again. I knew he could read my aura, but I was strong enough to dampen it, so to him I must have felt young. Even so, he was very foolish or he was working for someone very strong — possibly both. Since there are no more than five or six vampires on Earth who are stronger than I, I had little to fear.

"Get out," he ordered me.

"No," I replied, continuing toward the Café Sangra.

I heard him draw a gun, but he had no chance to aim before I was there. I twisted the gun sharply to the side, and he dropped it so that his wrist would not break. My prey's eyes went wide as she saw this, and she ran away blindly, darting around the corner. Stupid human.

I stopped veiling my aura, and my attacker's eyes went wide as he felt its full strength.

"Is that all you were armed with?" I scoffed. "You work for my kind — you must have more than one gun."

He went to draw a knife, but I grabbed it first and threw it into the street hard enough to slam an inch of steel into the ground.

"Who — Who are you?" he stammered, afraid.

"Who do you think I am, child?"

I tend to avoid most of my kind, and destroy those who insist on approaching. Because of this, few recognize me. "Whose are you?" I snapped when he did not immediately respond. I received only a blank stare in return.

I reached into his mind and tore out the information I wanted. Those of my line are the strongest of the vampires when it comes to using our minds, and never have I found a reason to avoid exercising that power. When I found what I sought, I threw the human away from me.

I swore as I realized who this human belonged to.

Aubrey . . . He is one of the few vampires stronger than I. He is also the only one who would care about my presence in his land.

I had been in this part of New York City before but had never encountered Aubrey or any of his servants here. Yet, according to this human, the place belonged to my enemy.

My attacker smiled mockingly. Perhaps he thought I was afraid of his master. Indeed, I fear Aubrey more than anything else on this Earth, but not enough to spare this boy. Aubrey would learn about my being on his territory one way or another, and this child was bothering me.

"Ryan," I crooned, finding his name as I read his mind. He relaxed slightly. I smiled, flashing fangs, and he paled to a chalky white. "You made me lose my prey."

Before he had a chance to run, I stepped toward him, placing a hand on the back of his neck. As I did so I caught his eye, whispering a single word to his mind: *Sleep.* He went limp, and did not fight as my fangs pierced his throat. I could taste a trace of Aubrey's blood in the otherwise mortal elixir that ran through Ryan's veins, and that taste made me shiver.

I did not bother disguising the kill. If Aubrey wished to claim that street, he could deal with the body and the human authorities. Either way, Aubrey would feel my aura and know I had been there; very few would dare to kill one of Aubrey's servants on his own territory.

Though I feared Aubrey and dreaded what would happen should I confront him again, I refused to show that fear. That was the first time our paths had crossed in nearly three hundred years. I would not show that I still feared him.

Aubrey . . . Hatred flickers through me at the thought of him.

The long-stemmed rose lies on the scarlet comforter over my bed, its petals soft, perfectly formed, and black.

I pick up the rose, cutting my hand on a thorn, which is as sharp as a serpent's tooth. I look at the blood for a moment as the wound heals, reminded of a time long ago; then absently I lick it away. My mind returns again to the time when I was still Rachel Weatere — a time when I was given another black rose.

Then I did not lick the blood away.

CHAPTER 4

1701

"Rachel," Lynette said to me. "You have a caller. Papa is waiting with him." Her tone reminded me of a pouting child.

Nearly a month had gone by since Lynette had been burned. My sister was unaware of Alexander's tortured mind; she knew nothing of the powers that he was so afraid of, and believed the fire to be an accident.

Alexander had not spoken to me again about the things he saw, though I recognized the moments when the visions surfaced in his mind. I alone noticed when his face went dark and his focus changed, as if he was listening to voices only he could hear.

When I reached the door, I saw what had made Lynette unhappy. The caller was a dark-haired, black-eyed young man whom I knew only vaguely. Lynette was fourteen, and she resented the attention the boys in town paid to me, though she would never have said so aloud.

Alexander was looking at the visitor with a dark gaze. I remembered his confession to me about the things he saw, and how he could hear the thoughts in minds around him. I was afraid to know what he was seeing and hearing now.

Turning away from my brother, I looked at our visitor. He wore black breeches and a crimson shirt. The color was too bold for the time; the dyes for such brilliant hues were expensive. The whole outfit had probably cost more than my entire wardrobe.

"Please come in," my papa was saying. "I'm Peter Weatere, Rachel's father, and this is my son, Alexander. This is my other daughter, Lynette," he added as we joined them. "And of course you know Rachel."

Papa assumed that, since our visitor had asked for me, he knew me. But I had seen him before only in passing, and the one time I had spoken with him, I had not been told his name.

"Aubrey Karew," the young man introduced himself, shaking my father's hand. I heard the faintest trace of an accent, though

I could not place it. I had not been given much exposure to different languages.

I looked up, and Aubrey's eyes seemed to catch me. They sent shivers down my spine. Something kept me from looking away, as if I was a bird caught in the eyes of a snake.

"How may I help you, Mr. Karew?" my father was asking. I tried to keep my eyes down, as was proper, but could not. Aubrey's eyes were hypnotizing, and I could not force my gaze away from them.

Then this strange young man handed me a rose, which I took without thinking. I should not have been taking gifts from young men my father had barely met, but the way this man's eyes caught me had startled me, and I took the rose before I even realized what it was.

"Mr. Karew," my father said, frowning, "this is rather improper —"

"You're right," Aubrey said.

Papa stood dumbstruck. I looked at the rose, which I was still holding. It was beautiful — such long-stemmed roses did not grow in the northern colonies. For a moment I thought it was deep red, but soon I realized it was black. One of the thorns caught the skin of my hand, drawing blood, and I transferred the rose to my other hand, hoping no one had noticed.

I looked back up at Aubrey, whose eyes had fallen to the cut on my hand, and another shiver went down my back. He turned abruptly and left. He was gone before anyone could say a word.

My father turned to me, his face stern, but my brother intervened.

"It is too late to discuss our visitor rationally. We need to sleep before the bell rings for church tomorrow." I knew my brother well, and I recognized his tone: he did wish to discuss Aubrey, but not with my father. Papa nodded; he respected my brother.

Alexander had been the only one in my family who noticed my cut. After my father left, he took me out to the well to wash it, his expression worried.

"What is wrong, Alexander?" I asked him, still holding the rose, though I hardly noticed that I was doing so. "You look as if our guest had a serpent's tongue."

"Perhaps he did," Alexander said, his voice hushed and dark. "A black-eyed boy we have never seen comes to our door and offers you a black rose. You take his gift and cannot seem to put it down, even after it has drawn blood from you."

"What are you saying?" I whispered, shocked.

"I may not have signed the Devil's book, but that does not mean there are not creatures out there who belong to him."

"Alexander!" I whispered, shocked by the implication. He had all but accused this Aubrey Karew of being one of the Devil's creatures.

I looked at the rose, which was still in my hand, and then put it deliberately on the ground, trying to convince my brother — and perhaps myself — that such an action was possible.

Even so, my gaze remained on its black petals, and I realized how Alexander had felt when I told him to speak to a cleric after Lynette's accident. What would be said should I explain to a preacher about the black rose I had accepted? After all, I had heard that people signed the Devil's book with their blood, and my blood had been drawn.

Alexander walked back into the house silently, and I watched him leave, not knowing what to say. I could not deny that the rose was beautiful in a way — perfectly shaped, just opened. The color, though, was the color of darkness, death, and all the evil things I had been told of: black hearts, black art, black —

Black eyes. Hypnotic black eyes.

I did not like to believe that I might have accepted a gift from one of the Devil's creatures. I convinced myself that I had not.

Perhaps if I had believed —

Perhaps nothing. What could I have done?

The next day would be my last day in that world — my last day to speak to my papa, my sister, or my brother, and my last day to draw a breath and know that without it I would die. It would be my last day to thank the sun for giving light to my days.

I would argue with Alexander and avoid my papa. And, like all humanity, never once would I thank the sun or the air for its existence. Light, air, and my brother's love — I took them all for granted, and someone took them all away.

My last day of humanity . . . Rachel Weatere would die the next night.

CHAPTER 5

NOW

I pull my thoughts from the past, not wanting to dwell on that night, and my gaze again returns to the black rose. I wonder briefly where it was grown. It is so similar to the one Aubrey gave me three hundred years ago.

I hesitate to pick up the white florist's card that has been lying beneath the rose, but finally snatch it from the bed.

Stay in your place, Risika.

The rose is a warning. Aubrey did not like having his servant killed on his own land, and he is reminding me of my past.

I hunt in New York again this night, careful not to stray onto Aubrey's land but refusing to give up my favorite hunting grounds out of fear.

I stop in his part of New York for only a moment. I have burnt the card and leave the ashes in a plastic bag on the front step of the Café Sangra. I take orders from no one.

Some vampires, like some humans, know nothing other than submission. They do not wish to rise in power. But those vampires are rare. Few vampires will allow themselves to show fear of another, for as soon as you are proved weaker you become the hunted. The hunter hates being hunted, chased, or wounded. If it did not, it would not be an aggressive hunter, and those who cannot be aggressive are hunted down while they shiver and hide because the night is dark.

Forever is too long to live in fear.

Even so, I do not go to see Tora this night. I do not wish to draw Aubrey's attention to her until he has forgotten this small challenge. Although I resent being kept away from her, I would rather stay away than have her die so that my pride may be appeased. For Tora, I allow myself to fear Aubrey.

After I hunt, I change to hawk form and return to Concord, my mind still troubled. I fall into bed for the day, but I do not dream — I simply remember.

Chapter 6

1701

Alexander avoided me the day after Mr. Karew visited. We attended morning services as a family, but the rest of the day, Alexander mostly stayed in his room. During the short time he was out he looked dazed, as if he was seeing something I could not see or hearing voices I could not hear. Perhaps he was. I still do not know, and I never will.

When he approached me that evening, the dazed look was gone, replaced by determination.

"Rachel?"

"Yes?"

"I need to speak to you," Alexander told me. "I do not know how to explain to you so that you do not think . . ." He paused, and I waited for him to continue.

"There are creatures in this world besides humans," Alexander went on, his voice gaining strength and determination, "But they are not what the witch hunters say they are. The witches . . ." Again Alexander paused, and I waited for him to decide how to say what he needed to say. "I do not know if Satan exists — I have never seen him, personally — but I do know that there are creatures out there that would damn you if they could, simply for spite."

This was nothing I had not heard before at church. But my brother said it differently than the preacher ever did. I would say it sounded as if Alexander had more faith, but that wasn't quite it. It sounded as if, in his mind, he had proof.

"Alexander, what has happened?" I whispered. His words seemed a warning, but it was not a warning I understood.

Alexander sighed deeply. "I made a mistake, Rachel." Then he would say no more about it.

I went to bed that night feeling uneasy. I was afraid to know what Alexander's words meant, but even more afraid because I did not know.

Around eleven I heard footsteps moving past my door, as if someone was trying without success to move quietly. I rose silently, so as not to wake Lynette, with whom I shared the room, and tiptoed to the door.

I left my room and entered the kitchen, where I caught a glimpse of Alexander leaving by the back door. I began to follow him, wondering why he was sneaking out of the house at such a late hour.

I well knew the abstract look that I had glimpsed on his face: he had seen something in his mind. Whatever vision had driven him from sleep had scared him, and it pained me that he had walked straight past my door, not even hesitating, not willing to confide in me.

Alexander had slipped through the back door, but I hesitated beside the doorway, hearing voices behind the house. Alexander was speaking with Aubrey and a woman I did not know. Her accent was different from Aubrey's, but again it was not familiar to me. I did not know then that she had been raised to speak a language long dead.

The woman Alexander was speaking with had black hair that fell to her shoulders and formed a dark halo around her deathly pale skin and black eyes. She wore a black silk dress and silver jewelry that nearly covered her left hand. On her right wrist she wore a silver snake bracelet with rubies for eyes.

The black dress, the jewelry, and most of

all the red-eyed serpent, brought one word to my mind: *witch.*

"Why should I?" she was asking Alexander.

"Just stay away," he ordered. He sounded so calm, but I knew him well. I caught the shiver in his voice — the sound of anger and fear.

"Temptation," the woman said, pushing Alexander. He fell against the wall, and I could hear the impact as his back hit the wood. But she had hardly touched him! "Child, you would regret ordering me away from your sister," the woman added coldly.

"Do not hurt her, Ather." It was the first time I had heard her name, and shivers ran down my spine upon hearing my brother speak it. My golden-colored brother did not belong in the dark world she had risen from.

"I mean it," Alexander said, stepping forward from the wall. "I am the one who attacked you — leave Rachel be. If you need to fight someone to heal your pride, fight me, not my sister."

When I heard this, my heart jumped. Alexander was my brother. I had been born with him and raised with him. I knew him, and I knew he would not harm another human being.

"You and that witch should not have interrupted my hunt," said Ather.

"You should be grateful 'that witch' helped me stop you. If you had killed Lynette —"

"Which sister matters more to you, Alexander — your twin, or Lynette? You drew blood; you should have remembered Rachel before you did."

"I will not let you change her," Alexander growled.

"Why, Alexander," Ather said, advancing on him again. "What gave you the idea I wanted to change her?" She smiled; I saw her teeth as the moonlight fell on them. Then she laughed. "Just because she accepted my gift?" Ather took another step toward Alexander, and he stepped back. She laughed again. "Coward."

"You are a monster," Alexander answered. "I will not allow you to make Rachel one too."

"Aubrey," Ather said. Nothing more. Aubrey had been standing quietly in the shadows. He laughed and moved behind Alexander, but my brother did not react. He seemed unafraid to have Aubrey at his back.

"Rachel, do come join us," Ather called to me. I froze. I had not realized she had seen me. Ather nodded to Aubrey, who took a step in my direction, as if he might escort me into the yard. I did not step back from him but became angry instead.

"Get away from me," I spat. I had always been outspoken for my time, and Aubrey blinked in surprise. He stepped to the side and allowed me to walk past him toward Ather.

Alexander had said he had made a mistake. Now he was trying to protect me from the two who had come to avenge that mistake. I stalked past Aubrey to where Ather was standing.

"Who are you?" I demanded. "What are you doing here?"

"Rachel," she purred in greeting, ignoring my questions. She showed fangs when she smiled, and I was reminded of the serpent on her bracelet.

"Rachel, do not get angry," Alexander warned me.

"Too late." I spat the words into Ather's face. "Why were you threatening him?"

"Do not demand answers from me, *child*," Ather snapped.

"Do not call me child. Leave my property, now, and leave my brother alone."

Ather laughed. "Does this creature truly mean so much to you?" she asked me.

"Yes." I did not hesitate to answer. Alexander was my twin brother. He was part of my family, and I loved him. He had been cursed with a mixture of too much faith and damnable powers. He did not deserve the taunting he was receiving.

"That's unfortunate," Ather said dryly, and then, "Aubrey, will you deal with that distraction?" I started to turn toward Aubrey, who had drawn a knife from his belt, and barely saw him grab my brother before Ather took my head in both her powerful hands and forced me to look into her eyes. "Now he means nothing."

I heard Aubrey laugh, and then stop. I thought I heard a whisper, but it was so soft, so quick, that it could have been the wind. Aubrey reentered my line of vision, sheathing his blade. Then he disappeared, and I was left watching the place where he had stood. I stared after him, in shock perhaps. I heard nothing anymore, felt nothing.

Then what had just happened seemed to hit me, and I tried to turn to my brother, who was so silent — too silent. . . .

Ather grabbed my arm.

"Leave him there, Rachel," she told me.

But Alexander was hurt, maybe dying. I had no doubt Aubrey had drawn the knife to kill him. How could she tell me

39

to leave him? He needed help.

"I said, *leave him*," Ather whispered, once again turning me toward her. I stepped back, meeting her black eyes.

Cold shock was beginning to fill my mind, blocking the way of terror and pain. My brother could not be dead — not this suddenly.

"Do you know what I am, Rachel?" Ather asked me, and the question jolted me from my silent world. *This* was reality — not Alexander's death, not black roses. I could deal with this moment, so long as I did not think of the one before.

"You appear to be a creature from legend," I said carefully, worried about the consequences my words might have.

"You are right." Ather smiled again, and I wanted to slap that smile from her face. I remembered Alexander's words — *I am the one who attacked you* — and my surprise at hearing them. I could not believe my brother would ever harm anyone. The idea that such violence was in *me* was shocking . . . yet also strangely exciting.

Ather continued before I could say anything.

"I want to make you one of my kind."

"*No*," I told her. "Leave. Now. I do not want to be what you are."

"Did I say you had a choice?"

I pushed her away with all my strength, but she barely stumbled. She grabbed my shoulders. Long-nailed fingers twining in my hair, she tilted my head back and then leaned forward so that her lips touched my throat. The wicked fangs I had glimpsed before pierced my skin.

I fought; I fought for the immortal soul the preachers had taught me to believe in. I do not know whether I ever believed in it — I had never seen God, and He had never spoken to me — but I fought for it anyway, and I fought for Alexander.

Nothing I did mattered.

The feeling of having your blood drawn out is both seductive and soothing, like a caress and a gentle voice that is in your mind, whispering *Relax*. It makes you want to stop struggling and cooperate. I would not cooperate. But if you struggle, it hurts.

Ather's right hand pinned both of mine together behind me, and her left hand held me by the hair. Her teeth were in the vein that ran down my throat, but the pain hit me in the chest. It felt as if liquid fire was being forced through my veins instead of blood. My heart beat faster, from fear and pain and lack of blood. Eventually I lost consciousness.

★ ★ ★

A minute or an hour later, I woke for a moment in a dark place. There was no light and no sound, only pain and the thick, warm liquid that was being forced past my lips.

I swallowed again and again before my head cleared. The liquid was bittersweet, and as I drank I had an impression of power and . . . not life or death, but time. And strength and eternity . . .

Finally I realized what I had been drinking. I pushed away the wrist that someone was holding to my lips, but I was weak, and it was so tempting.

"Temptation." The voice was in my ears and my head, and I recognized it as Ather's.

Once again I pushed away the wrist, though my body screamed at me for doing so. Ather was insistent, but so was I. I somehow managed to turn my head away, despite the pain that shot through me with each beat of my heart. I could hear my own pulse in my ears, and it quickened until I could hardly breathe past it, but still I pushed away the blood. I believed, for that second, in my immortal soul, and would not abandon it — not willingly.

Suddenly Ather was gone. I was alone.

I could feel the blood in my veins, entering my body, soul, and mind. I could not get my breath; my head pounded and my heart raced. Then they both slowed.

I heard my own heart stop.

I felt my breath still.

My vision faded, and the blackness filled my mind.

CHAPTER 7

NOW

Never before and never after have I felt the soul-tearing, mind-breaking pain I experienced that night. I have looked into the minds of willing fledglings; never have I seen my own pain reflected. My line's strength comes at a price, and the price is that pain. It has changed us all. One cannot be conscious throughout one's own death and not be changed.

Perhaps that was the worst part. Or perhaps the worst part of my story is yet to come.

The visions of my past linger in the present. Alexander's face floats in my mind, and I cannot seem to make it disappear. My two lives have nothing in common, and yet as I stand in this house I feel as if I have somehow been transported back to the past, before my brother was killed.

Seeking a diversion, I bring myself to New York City. I do not shift into hawk form. I simply bring myself away with the ability that only my kind has — the ability to change to pure energy, pure ether, for the instant it takes to travel in that form to another place. It takes me only a thought, and I arrive in less than a second.

I automatically shield my aura as I appear in the alley, not wishing to announce my presence to the world. Then I walk through the scarred wooden door that leads to Ambrosia, one of the city's many vampire clubs. This place was once owned by another of Ather's fledglings, a vampire named Kala. But Kala was killed by a vampire hunter. Yes, they do exist; witches and even humans often hunt our kind. I do not know who owns this place now that they have killed Kala.

The club is small and looks like any café — or it would if it had windows and more light than the single candle in the corner gives. Of course, I can see by the dim light, but a human would be close to blind in Ambrosia.

At the counter is another of my kind. I do not know him. He has his head down on the counter, and the skin I can see is almost gray. As I walk through the door he does not even look in my direction, though he does raise his head long enough to empty the glass that stands on the counter near him, and to lick the blood from his lips as a shiver wracks his body.

"Who did this to you?" I ask him, curious. There is no disease on Earth my kind can catch, and almost no poison that affects us, so I wonder why he looks ill.

"Some damn Triste," the stranger growls. "He was in the Café Sangra. I didn't even realize he wasn't human."

I wonder how Aubrey would react if he learned a Triste witch had been in the Café Sangra.

The Triste witches appear almost identical to humans. If one can read auras, their auras feel the same. Their hearts beat, and they breathe. They need to eat, just as humans do. Their blood tastes just like a human's.

However, they are not human in the least. Like vampires, Triste witches are immortal. They do not age, and their blood is poison to our kind. This child who chanced to feed off one is lucky he did not take much, or else he would already be dead.

"Since when does Aubrey allow Tristes in his territory?" I ask. The two kinds — vampires and witches — are usually enemies. The word *Triste* can almost be used as a synonym for *vampire hunter.*

"He doesn't. I was feeding," he answers, cringing a bit. "And then found myself on the floor with my arm broken. Aubrey tossed me away from the witch like some kind of a doll. They got into an argument, and the witch was thrown out. But this witch, he gave me this on the way out," he says, holding up a folded slip of paper. "Said to give it to some fledgling of Ather's."

He adds, "Ather doesn't have any fledglings called Rachel, does she?"

"*What?*" I gasp. I am the only one of Ather's fledglings who has ever been called by that name, and only Ather and Aubrey know it.

"He said, 'Give this to Rachel — Ather's fledgling.' "

I no longer wish to take the paper from his hand. I do not wish to know what it says. Rachel was human, weak, prey. Only Aubrey would call me by that name. Except for Ather, he alone knows all the memories it stirs, and he is the only one who would try to hurt me with it.

I am not Rachel, and I can never be Rachel again, I think. *Rachel is dead.*

I leave Ambrosia without another word, my head reeling with anger. I have seen Aubrey only twice since my death, and both times were long ago. Until recently, I have avoided him like bad blood.

When I return to my home at dawn, I find one of Aubrey's servants in my yard. This is my town, and I do not tolerate other vampires, or their servants, in my territory. This applies to Aubrey above all else, because he would take what is mine if I allowed it.

I change to human form less than a foot from the interloper and push him against the wall of the house.

"What do you want?" I demand.

"Aubrey sent —"

I have no patience and reach into his mind, finding the information I want. Aubrey sent him to warn me away again. If Aubrey had come himself we would have fought, and while I know he does not fear challenging me, I cannot see us fighting again without one of us dying.

"Tell him I hunt where I wish," I say to the human. "And I will kill any other servants of his who approach me." It is dangerous to send such messages to another vampire. What I have said is very close to a challenge — one I hope to avoid — but so be it. If I must, I will play thin ice with Aubrey tonight. I do not care that if the ice breaks it will be I who falls through.

I leave the human on the doorstep and return to my room.

CHAPTER 8

1701

I felt myself die. I remember hoping I would wake again, that somehow I would live, but then I realized what that would mean.

I was dead.

I threw myself into the shadows of death and became lost.

Senses and memories came slowly when I first awakened.

I remembered a death, and I remembered that it had been I who had died, but I did not remember who that "I" was.

Trying to open my eyes, I saw only blackness. I thought I was blind, and that terrified me. Was this death, then? Floating forever in blackness, not even remembering who you had been?

As that thought brushed my mind I realized I was not floating. No — I could feel a wooden floor beneath me, and I was leaning against a wall that was cold and smooth like glass. I groped blindly around myself but felt nothing else. Behind me was the glass wall, and in front of me was only blackness.

I forced myself to my feet. Though all my muscles were stiff, after a moment I was able to stand.

I felt for my pulse and could not find it. I tried to shout and realized I did not have air in my lungs to do so. No heartbeat. No breath. I became afraid once again. I was dead, wasn't I? If not, what was I?

Humans breathe when alive, even when they are asleep or unaware of their breathing. Since waking, I had not taken a breath, and I had not noticed until now.

I finally tried to draw a deep breath, but sharp pain shot through my lungs. It knocked me to my knees, then slowly began to fade. Finally it subsided, and I tried to speak, wondering if I would be able to hear myself. Are not the dead both deaf and mute?

I took another tentative breath, and the pain did not strike as hard this time, so I used the breath to ask the darkness, "Can anyone hear me?" I received no reply, and I did not wish to ask again.

I tried to ignore my fear, working the stiffness from my joints and forcing myself to take another breath. The pain was almost gone, but my ribs still felt sore, as if the muscles around them had not been used for a long time. I felt no need to exhale, and I did not become dizzy when I did not do so. Letting out the unnecessary breath, I marveled when my body did not tell me to take another.

I had my senses of touch and hearing. I could speak. I could taste, and the taste in my mouth was sweet and vaguely familiar. I licked my lips and found that it was there as well. A memory tried to surface in my mind, one of pain and fear. I did not want it, so I pushed it away.

I tried to determine whether I could smell anything in the darkness. A honey-like scent wafted in the still, cool air. Beeswax? A candle, perhaps? I could also smell the light, dry scent of wood and an even fainter scent like frost — glass. It did not occur to me that I should not be able to smell *glass*. No human could.

Beneath these scents was something I did not recognize — not really like a smell at all, but like something between a taste and a fragrance that you catch for a moment on the breeze. Or perhaps it was the breeze itself, a gentle movement in the air. I focused on this sensation, and though it did not become clearer, its presence was strong.

Later I learned that this feeling was aura. The aura of death — my death — and of a vampire: Ather, my dark, immortal mother, who gave me this life against my will and who killed my mortal self.

I tried to walk, searching for a way out of the black room I was in, and found it surprisingly easy. The stiffness was gone from my body, and I moved smoothly, more as if I was floating than walking. The wood beneath my bare feet was smooth and cool.

I followed the wall until I reached a place that was not glass — a wooden door. I opened it slowly and blinked at the light that poured in. Turning my face away, I caught sight of the room I had just left. All four walls were mirrored, and my reflection flew back at me hundreds of times. Amazement filled me. Whoever owned this house must be rich, to have so much glass in one room. And yet there were no windows at all: nothing to let in the light and air.

I walked back into the room, entranced by my own reflection, hardly recognizing myself. I approached the mirrored surface and stretched a tentative hand out to the stranger reflected there. Her hair was still my golden hair, and her body had nearly my body's shape, but her form was more graceful, and when she walked she seemed to glide effortlessly. Her eyes were black as midnight, her skin as pale as death.

"Look hard, Risika," a voice behind me said. "Remember it well, for soon it will fade."

I spun toward the voice. Everything about the speaker was black, from her hair and eyes to her clothing, everything but her unnaturally fair skin. My first thought was *witch*. It came from some vague recollection of my past life, though I did not know what that life had held.

My next thought was *Ather.* I remembered her — I remembered the dark halo her hair formed around her pale skin, and I remembered her icy laugh.

A scene flashed through my mind. Once again I remembered my death, but now I remembered before that — Aubrey, sheathing the knife that had just taken a life. Whose life? I did not know and was not sure I wanted to.

"Why have you brought me here?" I demanded. "What have you done to me?"

"Come, now," Ather told me. "Surely

you can figure it out. Look at my reflection — look well. Then tell me what I have done to you."

I obeyed her command and turned back to the mirror. I could barely see her reflection. In the glass her form was so faint that her black hair appeared as little more than pale smoke.

"Now look at your own reflection," she told me.

I did. Once again I looked at the figure in the mirror, wondering if she could truly be me. I had a picture of myself in my mind, and it was not the same as the one I was seeing; though very close, perhaps, it was still very wrong.

"Who am I?" I asked, turning back to her. I truly did not know.

"You do not remember your life?"

"No." Ather smiled as I responded. A cold smile — if a snake could smile, it would smile as she did.

"I thought so," she answered. "Your memory will, sadly, return later, but for now . . ." She trailed off with a shrug, as if it did not matter.

"Who am I?" I demanded. "Answer me." I was angry, but her nonchalance was not the only reason. My mind had been spinning since I awoke. The sensation had been faint at first, but now the edges of my vision were beginning to go red.

"Why?" she responded. "Who you were no longer matters. You are Risika, of Silver's bloodline."

"And who is Risika?" I pressed, trying to ignore the painful shiver that wracked my body. "What is she?"

"She is — *you* are — a vampire," Ather told me. The information took a moment to reach my mind. I knew words like *witch* and *Devil*. This one was foreign. From somewhere, some memory I could not quite see, I heard someone say, *"There are creatures out there that would damn you if they could, simply for spite."*

Surely Ather was one of those creatures the speaker had been talking about. And Aubrey — I remembered him as well. Once again I saw him sheathing his knife, but still I could not remember why he had taken it out.

"You have made me into —" I broke off.

"Do you know I can read your mind like a book?" Ather said, laughing. "You are young now, still partially human. You will quickly learn to shield your thoughts, perhaps even from me. You are strong, even now. He warned me you would be. Was he afraid you would be too strong for me to control?"

I did not say anything, hardly understanding what Ather said. My head was
spinning as if I had hit it on something,
and I was having difficulty focusing on
anything.

Ather paused, looking at me, and then
smiled. When she did, I could see pale
fangs, and I repressed another shiver.
"Come, child," she told me. "You need to
hunt before your body destroys itself."

Hunt. The word sent dread through me.
It reminded me of wolves and cougars, animals who stalked their prey in the forest.
Blood soaking into the ground. So much
blood . . .

Now I wanted that blood. I could see the
scarlet death in my mind. Surely the blood
was warm and sweet and —

What was happening to me? These
thoughts were not mine, were they?

"Come, Risika," Ather snapped. "The
pain will worsen until you either feed or go
mad from it."

"No." I said the word solidly, without reluctance, despite the way I felt. I was
burning, and there was dust in my veins. I
thought of blood and craved it the way I
craved water on a long, hot day. I knew
what Ather meant when she said *hunt*, but
I would not kill to ease my own pain. I was

not an animal. I was a human being. . . .

At least, I hoped I was human. What had Ather done to me?

"Risika," she told me, "if you do not feed, the blood I have given you will kill you." She was not pleading with me; she was stating facts. "It will take days before you are truly dead, but by sunset tomorrow you will be too weak to hunt for yourself, and I refuse to spoon-feed you. Hunt or die, it is your choice."

I hesitated, trying to remember. There was a reason that I should not hunt. Someone I knew would have resisted, someone I loved but could not remember . . . I could not remember. The only reason I could remember now was the one I had been taught all my life by the preachers — because killing was a sin.

But dying by my own choice was a sin as well.

Perhaps I was already damned.

"Foolish child," Ather said. "Look at yourself in that mirror and tell me that your own church would not condemn you for what you are. Would you refuse the life I have given you to try to save the soul which your god has damned?"

"I will not sell my soul to save my life," I said, though in my mind I was not so sure.

My church was cold and strict, but I feared the nothingness of a soulless death just as much as I feared the flames of the spoken Hell. And perhaps she was right. Perhaps it was already too late.

"No," I said again, trying to convince myself more than her. "I will not."

"Brave words," Ather told me. "What if I told you it did not matter?" She was whispering now, as if that would drive her words into my mind. It was working. "You signed the Devil's book as your blood fell onto my gift to you."

In my mind the scene played itself out again. A black rose, the thorns sharp like the fangs of a viper. A drop of blood falling on the black flower as those fanglike thorns cut the hand that held them. Black eyes, much like Ather's black eyes but somehow infinitely colder, watching like a snake as the blood fell. Watching like a viper, like the thorns of the rose, as if he had bitten me . . .

My mind was filled with dark images and darker thoughts of snakes and hunting beasts and red blood falling on black petals. My heart was filled with pain and anger and hatred and the black blood that had damned me.

CHAPTER 9

NOW

I pull myself from my memories. I curse the fool I was to think I could save my damned soul with silly protests.

Aubrey's servant has run from my home, and I sense him leaving my town. He fears for his life, with good reason. Had he stayed I would have killed him. He knows I would, and he knows I can smell his fear.

I may have been changed against my will, but I do not fight what I am anymore. There is no greater freedom than feeling the night air against your face as you run through the forest, no greater joy than the hunt. The taste of your prey's fear, the sound of its heart beating strong and fast, the smells of the night.

I stand in this small town, so near to the dead and almost as near to the faithful in the church across the street, feeling the fear of the human running from my home. For that is what I am — a hunter. I learned long ago that I could not deny that fact.

Every instinct tells me to hunt this running, frightened creature. I am a vampire, after all. But I am not an animal, and I was once a human. That is what makes my kind dangerous: a hunter's instincts and a human's mind. Humanity's cruel way of toying with the world, laced with the savage, unthinking hunt of the wild animal.

But I do have control, and I will let this human live to tell his news to Aubrey, whom he fears even more than he fears me. He is the bearer of bad news, and Aubrey does not like bad news.

I refuse to allow Aubrey to rule me, but only because it is the way of my kind. I fear Aubrey as much as this human does, perhaps more, for I know exactly what Aubrey is and what he is capable of.

I am restless. Despite the rising sun, I am in the mood to do something.

After making a quick check to make sure there is no blood on me from the previous night's hunt, I leave my house. I walk, partly because I am not leaving Concord and thus not going far, but mostly because I have a craving to move.

Occasionally I visit cafés like Ambrosia, which cater to my kind. But more often I become a shadow of the human world. Human lives, which seem so complex to those who are living them, seem simple from the perspective of three hundred years.

The coffee shop has just opened when I slip through the door.

The girl who works there is human, of course. Her name is Alexis, and she has worked there for most of the summer.

"Morning, Elizabeth," she greets me, and I smile in return. I often visit this place in the morning. Of course, I did not give Alexis my real name. I do not allow myself to grow close to humans. They have a tendency to notice that I never age.

I buy coffee, not because I want the caffeine or even like the taste, but because people will stare at someone who is sitting in a coffee shop without anything to drink.

A few minutes later the prework traffic begins. For about half an hour the shop bustles, and I sit in the corner silently and watch people.

Though I have worked to distance myself from human society, I enjoy watching humans as they go about their business.

The principal of the nearby school hurries in, already late for work, dressed in a somber suit that makes her look even more tired than she is. A minute later a middle-aged man opens the door, stopping in during his morning jog. Two women, sipping their coffee at one of the small tables, get into a quiet argument over an article one read in the newspaper. A teenage girl meets her boyfriend and then is horrified as her father walks into the coffee shop.

I smile silently, watching the various dramas, which will probably be forgotten by evening.

Business slows as the customers depart, many complaining about their destination.

Humans are often this way. They go about their lives, constantly working, complaining of boredom one minute and overwork the next. They pause only to observe the niceties of society, greeting each other with "Good morning" while their minds are somewhere else completely.

Sometimes I wonder what my life would be like if I had been born into this modern time. Sin and evil no longer seem as important as they did three hundred years ago. Would I have been as horrified at what I have become, I wonder, if I had not been raised in the church, with the ever-present threat of damnation?

The two women in the corner who have been arguing about politics now stand and depart together, laughing. I watch them with an ounce of jealousy, knowing their worries are far away and that despite everything they know, they are still innocent.

Innocence . . . I remember when the last of my innocence died.

CHAPTER 10

1701

Ather led me from her house, and I saw no choice but to follow. The moonlight cleared my mind slightly, but my vision was still red around the edges, and my head was pounding.

I did not have specific memories of who I had been, but I knew what a town was, and what a house was. And everything I saw around me was somehow not *right*.

Ather's home was at the fringe of a wood, set far back from the road. After a moment I realized what was bothering me about it: the house was painted black with white shutters, as was the one next door. I had an impression of inversion, like the black Masses I had been told of at which Devil-spawns spoke the Lord's Prayer backward. It was the same, and so very wrong.

"Where are we?" I finally asked.

"This place does not exist," Ather answered. I frowned, not understanding. She sighed, impatient with my ignorance. "This town is called Mayhem. It is as solid as the town you grew up in, but our kind owns it, and no one outside even knows it exists. Stop thinking about things you need not worry about, Risika. You need to feed."

You need to feed. I shut my eyes for a moment, trying to blink away the burning sensation. I shook my head, but the pain refused to dull. Would I need to kill to sate it? I did not want to kill, but I did not want to die, but I did not want to kill. . . . What happened to the damned when they died?

"No," I said again, though this time it meant nothing in my ears and nothing in my mind. Thinking was impossible. I only knew I did not want to kill, but all I could think about was blood . . . red blood on black petals, and thorns and fangs like a viper's . . . .

The pain was intense, pushing my reason away from me, and my thoughts were no longer coherent. Ather sounded so sure, so calm.

"Come, child," she said soothingly. "You can feed on one of the witches waiting for death, if that would appease your conscience. They are already doomed to death and worse."

A shiver wracked my body, and the pain in my eyes and head grew. My hands were numb.

I am not sure whether I nodded. I believe I may have.

The next instant I found myself in a cold, dark cell with two of the accused witches. I did not consciously know how I arrived there, but part of me knew that Ather had used her mind to move us both. She appeared beside me a moment later.

I heard a beating that filled the room, and it took me a moment to realize that it was the heartbeats of the two women who were in the cell with us. One of them had screamed when she saw us, and the other had crossed herself. The smell of fear was sharp, and though I had never smelled it before, I recognized the scent the way a wolf does.

The accused witches tried to move away from us, one reciting the Lord's Prayer, the other still screaming. But the cell was too small for them to go far. I hardly heard the prayer.

I was aware only of their heartbeats and the pulses in their wrists and throats. I heard nothing else, saw nothing else. My vision was red-hazed, and my head was spinning.

Feed freely. I recognized Ather's voice in my mind. She smiled at me, and I caught a flash of fang. Absently I brushed my tongue over my own canines and realized that they were the same — too sharp, too long, they did not belong in a human mouth. I could feel the tips, vicious as a snake's, pressing into my lower lip.

I saw Ather walk toward the still screaming woman, who quieted and went limp, as if she had fallen asleep. Ather pulled back the woman's head, exposing the pulse in her neck. Ather's razor-sharp fangs neatly broke the woman's skin, and the scent of blood entered the room.

I lost all ideas of sin and murder then.

I lost all that had once made me Rachel.

I turned to the other woman, whose prayer had become a babble.

I fed.

I tasted her life as it flowed into me. Ather's blood had been cool and filled with the essence of immortality. This human's blood was thick and hot, boiling with pure life and energy. It wet my parched mouth and brought down my fever, and I drank it like a healing ambrosia.

Flashes of thought came to me, too fast for me to realize at first that they were not my own. After a moment I gained more control and discovered they were from my victim. I saw a laughing human child. It called to its mother to show her a flower. I saw a dinner cooking in a hearth. I saw a wedding. I saw morning services. My mind focused on this last image.

I could see this woman's mind clearly, and she was innocent of any form of witchcraft. This thought, more than any other, caused a complete change in me. This woman had been sent here to die as a witch, and she was innocent of the crime. Why had her own people accused her? How many more of the accused were innocent?

I tried to draw away quickly, but I moved as if under water. It was so tempting to drink for just a moment more, and a moment more than that, and just a moment more . . .

"And lead us not into temptation." I had spoken those words without faith so many times. If true belief had backed my prayer, would the words have been rewarded? Or would I still have been in that cell, feasting on the blood of an innocent woman?

All I knew at that time was that I did not

want to kill, and yet I could not draw away. Even as I heard her heart stop and felt the flow of blood slowing, even as she died, it was hard to stop feeding. My vision returned as her vision faded, and I looked at the innocent woman, now pale as chalk and empty of blood.

Beside me Ather licked her lips and dropped her prey to the stained, dirty floor of the cell. She looked as satisfied as a kitten with a bowl of cream. I was horrified, but not simply because of the killing. I had been unable to draw away as an innocent woman died, even though I could have saved her life.

"It is easy to kill, Risika," Ather told me. "And it gets easier the more you do it."

"No," I answered. How many times had I said that word in the past day? What meaning did it have anymore? I was not as sure as I wanted to be.

"You will learn," she told me, taking the woman from my arms and dropping her to the ground with the other innocent. "You are a predator now, and survival is the only rule of a predator's world."

"I will not be a killer."

"You will," she said, walking behind me. I turned to keep her in my view. She sounded so sure, and I felt so unsure. "You are above the humans now, Risika, above even most of our kind. Will you let them rule you because that is how the humans taught you?"

I did not answer, because I could not do so without agreeing with her.

"The law of the jungle says 'Be strong or be dominated.' The law of our world says 'Be strong or be killed.' "

"It is not my world!" I shouted. I did not want to belong to this fierce world of hunters who fed on the blood of innocents.

"Yes, it is, Risika," Ather insisted.

"I won't let it be."

"You have no choice, child."

"You're evil. I won't kill because you tell me to —"

"Then kill because it is your right." She snapped each word off, impatient with my refusal. "You are no longer human, Risika. Humans are your prey. You have never felt sorrow for the chickens you killed so that they could grace your plate. The animals you raised so that they could be killed. The creatures you put in pens so that you could own them. Why should you feel differently toward your meal now?"

She put it in a way I could not disagree with. "But you can't just kill humans. It's —"

"Evil?" Ather finished for me. "The world is evil, Risika. Wolves hunt the stragglers in a group of deer. Vultures devour the fallen. Hyenas destroy the weak. Humans kill that which they fear. Survive and be strong, or die, cornered by your prey, trembling because the night is dark."

CHAPTER 11

NOW

I leave the coffee shop and return to my home before the sun rises too high for comfort.

I go to bed, fall into a deep sleep, and awaken that evening in a foul mood.

I allow myself to hide in fear. Even as I say I will not let Aubrey rule my life, I let him keep me from the one thing in this world that can still bring me joy: Tora, my tiger. My beautiful, pure-minded tiger, who was once free and is now caged.

Aubrey has stolen so much from me. I have sworn to avenge the lives he has taken, but every time I have been too much a coward to challenge him.

My mood is as dark as Aubrey's eyes, black without end, and I want to fight back. So I deliberately hunt in Aubrey's land — the dying heart of New York City, where the streets are darkened with shadows cast by the invisible world.

I see another of my kind, a young fledgling, in one of the alleys. She senses my strength and cowers, blinking away like a candle flame in the night.

She is weak and not a threat to Aubrey's claim on this dark corner of the city, so he tolerates her presence. Perhaps he shows off occasionally, simply to keep her afraid. But he knows she will never challenge him. I am Aubrey's own blood sister, created by the same dark mother. If he tolerates me I could be as much a threat to his position as a mongoose in a cobra's nest — not because I am stronger, which I am not, but because it will appear to others of our kind that he fears me, and his pride is too strong to allow that.

I hunt and leave my prey dying in the street. Perhaps it is foolish to bait Aubrey this way, but I have lived too long beneath his shadow and refuse to cower any longer. Aubrey himself does not challenge me as I feed, and my suspicions rise. Where is he, I wonder, that he does not know I am here? Or is it simply that he does not care? Is he that sure of his claim?

I return to my home in a dark mood, but

as I enter my room my thoughts turn to ice.

I can sense the aura of one of my kind, one of my kin, and I recognize it very well. Aubrey. Aubrey with black hair and black eyes, Aubrey who saw the blood falling from my hand and smiled, Aubrey who laughed when he killed my brother.

Aubrey is the only vampire I know who prefers using a knife to using his mind, teeth, or hands. I touch the scar I bear on my left shoulder, the scar given to me only a few days after I died, created by the same blade that took my brother's life. The scar that I swore, on the day it was dealt, to avenge, along with my brother's death.

Chapter 12

1701

After the day when I lost my mortal soul, I never went back to my old home. I understood I no longer belonged there. I hated to think what my papa was going through, but I hated even more the idea of his learning what I had become. I wanted him to believe me dead, because it was better for him to think I had simply disappeared than for him to know he had lost his daughter to a demon.

I fed on one of the true monsters — one of the many "witch hunters" who interrogated and jailed the accused, seeking guilt where there was none.

How humans can do such things to their fellows is beyond me. They torture, maim and kill their own kind, saying it is God's will.

I no longer try to understand the ways of

humanity. Of course, maybe I'm being hypocritical. My kind is often just as cruel to our own. We are simply more direct. We need no one else to blame our violence on. If I kill Aubrey, I will do so because I hate him, not because he is evil, or because he kills, or for any other moral reason. I will do so because I wish to do so, or I will not do so because I do not wish to.

Or I will not do so because he kills me first, which is the end I expect.

Soon after I was transformed, I brought myself up to the Appalachian Mountains for a time. I had been told about them, yet had never seen them. It was incredible to be in the mountains at night. I was a young woman, alone in the wilderness. Had I been still human, such a thing would never have been allowed. I lay in a treetop, listening to the forest and thinking about nothing at all.

"Ather has been looking for you," someone said to me, and I jumped down to the ground. My prey lay beneath the tree. I had taken him to this place with my mind before I fed, to avoid interruptions.

I walked toward the voice. It was Aubrey.

"Tell Ather I do not want to see her," I said to him.

Aubrey was dressed differently than when I had last seen him, and could no longer be mistaken for a normal human. He had a green viper painted on his left hand, and was wearing a fine gold chain around his neck with a gold cross suspended from it. The cross was strung on the chain upside down.

He held his knife in his left hand. The silver was clean, sharp, and so very deadly, just like his pearl white viper fangs, which were, for the moment, hidden.

"Tell Ather yourself — I'm not your messenger boy," he hissed at me.

"No, you just take Ather's orders, like a good little lapdog."

"No one orders me, child."

"Except Ather," I countered. "She snaps and you jump. Or search, or kill."

"Not always . . . I just didn't like your brother," Aubrey answered, laughing. Aubrey smiles only when he is in the mood to destroy. I wanted to knock every tooth out of that smile and leave him dying in the dirt.

"You laugh?" I ask. "You murdered my brother, and you laugh about it?"

He laughed again in response. "Who was that carrion on the ground behind you, Risika?" he taunted. "Did you even bother to ask? Who loved him? To whom was he a brother? You stepped over his body without a care. *Over the body* — no respect, Risika. You would leave his body here without a prayer for the scavengers to eat. Who is the monster now, Risika?"

His words stung, and I instantly tried to defend my actions. "He —"

"He deserved it?" Aubrey finished for me. "Are you a god now, Risika, deciding who is to live and who is to die? The world has teeth and claws, Risika; you are either the predator or the prey. No one deserves to die any more than they deserve to live. The weak die, the strong survive. There is nothing else. Your brother was one of the weak. It is his own fault if he is dead."

I hit him. I had been a young lady, not taught to fight, but in that minute I was simple fury. I hit him hard enough to snap his head to the side and send him stumbling. He righted himself, the last of the humor gone from his face.

"Careful, Risika." His voice was icy, a voice to send shivers through the bravest heart, but I was too angry to notice.

"Do not speak of my brother that way."

My voice shook with rage, and my hands clenched and unclenched. "Ever."

"Or what?" he asked quietly. His voice

had gone darker, colder, and he was standing as still as stone. I could feel his rage cover me like a blanket. I knew in that instant that if anyone had ever threatened Aubrey, they were no longer alive to tell of it.

There was a first time for everything.

"I will put that blade through your heart, and you will never speak again," I answered.

He threw the knife down so that it landed an inch from my feet, its blade embedded in the ground.

"Try it."

I knelt slowly and cautiously to get the knife, not moving my eyes from Aubrey, who was watching with an icy stillness. I did not know what he would do, but I knew he would not simply let me kill him. Yet he stood there, silent, still, and faintly mocking in his expression, and did nothing.

"Well, Risika?" he prompted. "You said you would — now do it. You hold the knife. I stand defenseless. Kill me."

If I had killed him then . . . If I had been able to murder him then . . .

"You can't," he finally said, when I did not move. "You can't kill me while I am defenseless because you still think like a human. "Well, know this, Risika — that isn't how the world works."

He grabbed my wrist with one hand and my throat with the other. The knife was useless.

"Ather talks about you as if you are so strong. You're just as weak as your brother is."

I had never learned any fighting skills. I had never practiced violence. But in nature survival is the name of the game, and the body touches its long-dead roots. You adapt, because if you cannot, you're as good as dead. I adapted.

I wrenched my wrist from Aubrey's grip while using my free hand to push away the hand that held me. The knife fell, forgotten. My wrist was broken, but there was little pain — the vampire's tolerance for pain is high, and the injury was healing quickly.

I felt a spinning, burning sensation and failed to see Aubrey's next attack. He pounced, knocking me back over the tree roots and onto the ground. I kicked his kneecap with all my strength, breaking it. He hissed in pain and anger, falling to the ground. I started to push myself up, but pain lanced through my arms and back.

A fight between two vampires may look

physical, but when they are as strong as my line is, most damage is done with the mind. A strong vampire can strike out with its mind and kill a human without even touching it. It is harder to kill another vampire, but the fighters can still distract and disable each other. I was young and did not know how to fight that way. I was on the ground and couldn't push myself up because of the pain.

Aubrey was there in a moment. He placed one hand on my throat, pinning me to the ground on my back. Even wounded he was far stronger than I.

He had retrieved the knife and held it against my throat.

"Remember this, Risika — I have no love for you. I think you are weak, and I don't care about your morals. If you challenge me again, you will lose."

I spat in his face. He drew the knife across my left shoulder, from the center of my throat, in the gap between the two collarbones, to the center of my upper left arm. I gasped. It burned like fire and hurt more than anything I had ever felt.

Most human blades will not scar our kind, but Aubrey's blade was not a human blade. Magic, for lack of a better word, was embedded deep in the silver. I learned later that Aubrey had taken his blade from a vampire hunter during his third year as a vampire. Its original owner had been raised as a vampire hunter, but even so he had lost to Aubrey.

Aubrey disappeared as I lay on the ground, riding out the pain. If the blade had been human silver, the wound would have healed in moments; instead it took some time for my body even to get control of the pain.

Once it had subsided from blinding to simply unbearable, I sat up slowly, gingerly tracing the wound. The bleeding had already stopped, but the wound did not close fully until after I had fed again. And it left a scar. My skin was already so pale that the scar showed only as a faint pearl-colored mark, but I knew where it was, and I could see it easily.

Somehow, though I knew not how, and someday, though I knew not when, I would avenge that scar and all that it stood for: Alexander's death, the death of my faith in humankind, and the death of Rachel, innocent Rachel, a human filled with illusion.

My kind can live forever. I would have a long time, and many opportunities, to keep that vow.

CHAPTER 13

NOW

I was foolish to attack him then, and am equally foolish to bait him now, but I have no other choice. I refuse to roll over and let Aubrey be king without ever challenging him.

I can sense his aura in the room but cannot see him, and he has not spoken.

Where are you, Aubrey? I ask him with my mind. *Why do you hide from me?*

I hear his laughing, taunting voice in my head; it is a voice I have come to hate with all my mind, all my strength, and all my soul. He says only four words, not even a sentence.

One line of a poem.

Tiger! Tiger! Burning bright . . .

I scream the wordless cry of the eagle, the hunting cry of the diving hawk, the angered cry of a caged beast, and I hear

Aubrey laugh in my mind. I know where he was as I hunted on his land.

Even as he laughs I change my shape to a golden hawk that flies from that room in her animal rage and lands inside the tiger's cage at the zoo. The sign, *"Panthera tigris tigris,"* has fallen, and its wooden post is snapped in two like a twig. The metal bars of the tiger's cage are bent. The guard is lying on the ground, pale and motionless.

I do not care about the guard or the sign, only about Tora, the one creature I have loved since Alexander's death. Tora, who is lying on her side, her paws bound, with a knife in her heart. She was born free, and deserved to live so. Instead she lived in a cage and was killed, bound and helpless. This more than anything makes me feel as if the knife was planted in my own heart instead of hers.

I shift back into my usual form and pull the knife from her, screaming another wordless cry of rage and grief. Tearing the ropes from her paws, I weep at each golden hair that has fallen from her and at each black hair that has forever lost its shine. I weep — weep as I did not when I lost my brother and my life. I weep until my thoughts run dark and my tears run dry.

Love is the strongest emotion any creature can feel except for hate, but hate can't hurt you. Love, and trust, and friendship, and all the other emotions humans value so much, are the only emotions that can bring pain. Only love can break a heart into so many pieces.

The greatest pain I have ever felt rode on the back of love. I loved Alexander, and every injury he received seemed reflected onto me. His death tore my heart out and bled it dry, and now Aubrey has used my love for Tora to push the blade in deeper.

This is why, I have learned, the strongest of the vampires keep all these emotions at arm's length: because they are weaknesses, and if you have weaknesses you can be taken down with all the other prey.

Close to dawn I lift my head, my long golden hair blending with Tora's tiger fur. I do not think, but add the black stripes to my own tiger-gold hair.

"Look, my beautiful," I whisper. "I have stolen your stripes. I will wear them so that your beauty will not be forgotten. My tiger, my Tora, my beautiful — I will not allow this crime to go unpunished." My eyes are dry but sparkle with anger and determination. "I will be sure he is truly dead before he takes another life I love."

I am focused inward, on Tora, and hear no

one approach me. However, I feel a brush of air against my hair, the aura of some visitor. My head snaps up, but I see no one. Whoever was there is gone, leaving nothing save a slip of paper next to my hand.

I pick up the paper, my eyes caught on the name that is scrawled across the top in black ink: *Rachel.* I cannot read the words below, which have run together where water has fallen onto the ink. *Not water, I* think, realizing how strongly the aura is mixed in with them — *tears.*

I stare at the name for a moment, then crush the note in my hand, a fine tremor of rage going through me at this creature who dares to taunt me so. I do not recognize the aura on the paper; I do not know who sent it.

"Rachel is dead," I say aloud. "I am not Rachel — she died three hundred years ago."

The tearstains on the paper — whose are they? What human learned of Rachel and was so pained by her story that he sent me this? Or is this note a sick joke of Aubrey's, another way to scar my heart?

"I don't want your games!" I shout. If the one who left this reminder is still near, let him confront me.

No one answers.

CHAPTER 14

NOW

My past and my present have combined to taunt me. Shaking with grief and anger, I return to Ambrosia. I glance around the room, checking for Aubrey. I do not see him.

I come to this place seeking a diversion. The ghost of Rachel cannot follow me here.

I see my image reflected in a crystal glass someone has left on a counter. My reflection is a misty apparition, but I can see Tora's markings in my hair and I laugh. This is something Aubrey will never take from me.

In this moment I feel like exactly what I am: a wild child of the darkness. A dangerous shadow in a mood to make trouble.

I look around the room again. Smiling, I toss my tiger-striped hair back from my face and perch on the counter. The girl behind it, a younger fledgling, opens her mouth as if to tell me to get down but then thinks better of it.

"What do you see, Tiger?" someone asks me, and I turn toward him. "You look around this room as if you saw it differently from all of us. What do you see?"

I recognize him, and I know he recognizes me. He is Ather's blood brother, Jager. People say he treats all life as a game that must be played — a cruel and deadly game in which whoever is winning makes the rules.

Jager appears eighteen, with dark skin and deep brown hair. His eyes are emerald green, and they reflect the dim light like a cat's. I know it is the same illusion as my hair. All vampires have black eyes, and Jager had dark eyes even when he was alive — he was born nearly five thousand years ago, in Egypt, and watched the great pyramids rise.

"I see someone who does not show his true eyes," I observe. "What do you see?"

"I see that my warnings to Ather and Aubrey were justified," he answers.

"Was it you who warned Ather I would be strong?"

"It was I who warned her that you would be stronger than she."

He sits on the counter beside me, and the girl behind it gives up, moving to a table on the other side of the room.

"Ather is weak," I comment. "It is one of her flaws. She changes those who will be stronger than her, because it makes others think she has more power than she does."

"She isn't the only one you are stronger than, Risika," he answers. "Aubrey isn't often challenged, because people know he is powerful, and they are afraid of him. He has you afraid of him, although he is not much stronger than you are, if at all."

"Oh, really?" I ask, not believing him. "Then we must be speaking of different Aubreys, because I lost the last time I fought the Aubrey I know."

"You could hide that scar with a thought. You have the power to do that," Jager says, changing the subject.

"I could," I answer. "But I don't."

"You wear it like a warning — a sign that you will avenge it."

"I will avenge more than this scar, Jager."

"When?" he presses. "Will you wait for him to start the music? Or will you start it yourself?"

"I prefer to kill in silence."

Jager gazes at me and smiles. "Happy

hunting, Risika." A moment later he is gone.

I lie back on the counter, thinking on his words, and then I too am gone. We are phantoms of the night, coming and going from the darkened city like shadows in candlelight.

I return to my home in a light, detached mood, not bothering with the complexities of revenge. I look out the front window, watching the few who are also returning to bed as the sun rises.

One of Concord's other shadows enters his house — a witch, but only by heritage, as he is not trained. He is not a threat to me.

I also see Jessica, Concord's young writer, looking out her own window. Jessica writes about vampires, and her books are true, though no one understands how she knows what she does. I wonder if I should tell her my story — perhaps she could write it for me. Perhaps it is my story she now writes.

I go upstairs and fall into bed and a vampiric sleep.

My dreams are my memories of the past. I dream of my years of innocence, while I was still fighting what I was.

CHAPTER 15

1704

I did not return to my home for three years, and when I finally did, no one saw me.

It was nearly midnight when I stopped in Concord, which was intentional. I did not wish to run into any humans.

I did not want to be recognized, of course, but more than that I was not sure I could control myself. The last time I had fed had been two nights previous, on a thief who had the ill luck to attack me as I wandered the darkened streets. The thirst beat at me viciously.

Though I consoled myself by saying I only killed those who deserved it, Aubrey's words always echoed in my mind: *Are you a god now, Risika, deciding who is to live and who is to die?* Thieves and murderers sustained me, but only just. I fed only as often as I needed to in order to survive, and the hunger was always near.

I stood outside the house I had once lived in, perched on the edge of the well, watching the house like a ghost, able to see and hear but unable to do anything else.

Would he recognize me, even if he saw me? The three years had changed me. My fair skin was frosty white, and my golden hair was tangled, not having seen a comb in a while. I wore men's clothing, having lost my patience with long dresses as I explored the forests, mountains, and rivers of the country.

Of course I could have walked up to the door and asked my father if he knew who I was, but I would not. He would only be hurt more when I had to leave again. I would not let him know what I had become.

Lynette was asleep in her room, but my father was awake, and crying. He looked out the window, and though I knew he was looking in my direction, he did not see me. I had learned how to shield my existence from mortal eyes.

The tears on his face sent daggers into my heart. I had a powerful vision of Aubrey and Ather lying dead, with me standing above them. Would anyone weep if they were killed? I did not think so, but I would never have the chance to know. Aubrey had proved beyond any doubt that I would not be the one to give him death.

A woman drifted downstairs behind my father. Her dark hair was tied back, and even from this distance I could see that her eyes were chocolate brown. Her skin was not as fair as my mother's had been. When she put a hand on my father's shoulder, I could see that she did not have the graceful artist's hands my father had often described my mother as having.

"Peter, it's late. You need to sleep."

My father turned to her and gave a weak smile, and for an instant I felt an irrational urge to go inside and *shake* this woman. I had seen my father's thoughts, and I knew without a doubt that this stranger was his wife. Her name was Katherine. Had he married her trying to replace us? Did she even know about Alexander and me? Did she care?

These people were no longer my family, that I knew. But I could not help hating this woman for trying to take my place.

"Jealous?" someone said over my shoulder, and I swung around toward Aubrey, knowing that my eyes were narrowed with hatred. "If she bothers you that much, kill her."

"I am sure you would appreciate that," I hissed.

He laughed. "You have too many morals."

"And you have none," I snapped back, trying to keep myself from hitting him. I refused to leave while he was here, his attention on my father and this innocent woman.

Innocent woman . . . strange, how my opinion changed so quickly. As soon as Aubrey suggested I kill her, I felt the need to protect her.

"I have some morals, I suppose," he argued, though his voice was light. He had taken no offense at the accusation. "But none that interfere with the way I survive. Look at yourself, Risika — you can hardly preach the benefits of morality."

Though I did not hate myself for killing to survive, I feared that I would one day become as indifferent to murder as Aubrey was.

"If you came here to convince me to abandon my morals, you are wasting your time," I snapped.

"You are hardly my only motive for being here," he answered lazily.

My father and his wife had decided to get some air and were now sitting on the back porch, quietly discussing how the farm was doing, Lynette's suitors, and everything else except for the reason my father had been crying.

As if he could sense my gaze on him, my father turned toward me, but this time his eyes went wide, as if he could see me despite my efforts.

Standing, he took a step in my direction before his wife put a hand on his arm. "There's no one there, Peter," she insisted, and my father sighed.

"I could have sworn I saw her. . . ." He shook his head, taking a raspy breath.

"You could have sworn you saw her a few days ago, but she was not there. You thought you saw your son the week before that, but he was not there. They never are, Peter, and they never will be. Let them go."

My father turned about and went inside the house. Katherine closed her eyes for a moment and whispered a prayer.

Why did she not help him herself? Was she so blind that she could not see how much her words had hurt him?

Aubrey laughed beside me. "You *are* jealous."

I spun toward him again, losing my temper. "Could you go somewhere else?"

"I could," he said. "But this is more fun."

"Damn you."

He shrugged, then looked past me to my father's wife, who had just stood and moved toward the house.

She hesitated, then turned slowly, sensing eyes on her back.

"Leave her alone, Aubrey," I commanded.

"Why?"

Katherine looked up as if she had heard a sound, and then walked toward us, though I could tell that she did not really see Aubrey or me.

I clenched my fists, knowing that he was baiting me and knowing equally well that if he had set his mind on killing this woman, there was no way I could stop him.

Katherine gasped as Aubrey stopped hiding himself from her. She froze, eyes wide.

"Fine, Aubrey — you have made your point," I snapped, stepping between him and his prey. "Now leave."

"And what point would that be?" he inquired. "I do not share your reservations, Risika. I hunt when I wish, as I always have."

"Hunt somewhere else," I said. His eyes narrowed.

"Who . . . Wh-What do you want?" Katherine stammered, backing away from us. She was breathing quickly, and her heart was beating fast from fear.

Aubrey disappeared from where he stood and reappeared behind her. Katharine stumbled into him and let out a gasp.

Aubrey whispered into her ear and she relaxed. Then he reached up and gently pulled her head back, exposing her throat . . .

CHAPTER 16

NOW

I snap awake, instantly alert.

There is someone in the house, in the room.

I rise from my bed. "Why do you hide, Aubrey?" I ask the shadows. "Do you finally fear me? Are you afraid that if you challenge me again you will lose?" I know this is not Aubrey's fear, but I am in the mood to taunt, just as I know he is.

There is one taunt that almost guarantees a vampire's response: accusing him of being afraid.

"I will never fear you, Risika," Aubrey answers as his form coalesces from the shadows of the room.

"You should," I respond. Vampiric powers strengthen with strong emotions — hate, rage, love — and Aubrey brings all those emotions to the surface of my mind.

Despite my hatred, if I fight him I will lose. This is a lesson I learned well years ago. Aubrey is older, stronger, and much crueler.

For now, though, he lounges against the wall, throwing his knife into the air and catching it. Throwing, catching. Up, down. The faint light glints on the silver blade, and I have a sudden picture in my mind of Aubrey missing the knife, and of it slicing across his wrist.

He has modernized his style since the 1700s: he wears black jeans tucked into black boots, a tight red shirt that shows off the muscles of his chest, and a metal-studded dog collar. The green viper has been replaced by the world serpent from Norse mythology, which played a part in the destruction of the world. On his upper arm is the Greek Echidna, mother of all monsters, and on his right wrist is the Norse monster Fenris, the giant wolf who swallowed the sun.

I wonder what Aubrey will do when he becomes bored with these designs. Maybe cut them off with an ordinary knife. His flesh would heal in a matter of seconds. Maybe I could volunteer to help. . . . No one would mind if I "accidentally" cut his heart out in the process.

"Why are you here, Aubrey?" I finally ask, not willing to wait for him to speak.

"I just came to offer my condolences for the death of your poor, fragile kitten."

My body freezes with rage. Aubrey knows how to hurt me, and how to make me lose my temper. He has done so before.

I start to move toward him — to hit him, to make him hurt as much as I do.

"Careful, Risika," he says. Just two words, but I stop. "Remember what happened last time you challenged me."

"I remember," I growl. My voice is heavy with pain and rage. I do remember — I remember very well.

"You still wear the scar, Risika. I can see it even from here."

"I have not forgotten, Aubrey," I answer him. He wears the same face he had then: cold, aloof, slightly amused, slightly mocking. He knows what Tora meant to me, and I know that he has visited me to try to bait me into attacking him again.

I wonder what kind of life made Aubrey the way he is. A psychologist would love analyzing him. Aubrey knows exactly what to say and do to make those around him weep, laugh, beg, hate, love, fear, or anything else he wishes. I have seen brave men run in fear, humans wage wars, and vampire hunters turn on their own, all because of Aubrey.

He is far stronger than Ather, physically, mentally, and emotionally. As I have said, Ather's largest flaw is that she changes people who are strong — people who will be stronger than she is. She does this because, though others of our kind might challenge her alone, they assume that her fledglings would avenge the attack.

I may never understand why Ather decided that Rachel was a human who demanded her attention, but I do not hate my blood mother. She was the one who tore me from my human life, but she was also the one who forced me to look upon the darkness of humanity. Had it not been for her, I would have lived and died as prey and nothing else.

Though I would not lift a finger to defend my blood mother, I do not go out of my way to attack her.

Aubrey, on the other hand . . . Three hundred long years ago I knew that Aubrey was stronger than I, and indeed, I fought him and lost. I fear what will happen if we fight again. He eggs me on every time we meet, knowing well that I fear him. I hate him all the more because of that fear, and he knows this as well.

He is still waiting for my response to his taunt.

"Considering you killed Tora, your condolences aren't worth much," I tell him.

He raises his eyebrows questioningly.

"Don't look like that. I could feel your aura there, and even now I can smell her blood on you."

Aubrey just laughs.

"Get out of my house, Aubrey," I growl. I have no wish to fight him. I only want him to be gone.

"You don't seem in the mood for company," he comments. "I'll stop by again later, Risika."

I hear the implied threat but have no chance to reply before he disappears. He has accomplished what he came here to accomplish and has no reason to stay.

I remember my dream the night before, and my mind returns to it, my anger at Aubrey forcing me to remember the rest.

He did not kill Katherine. He only killed the remainder of what might have been my soul.

Chapter 17

1704

I refused to watch him kill her.

Ignoring the consequences, I jumped at Aubrey, tearing him away from Katherine. The woman stumbled, falling to the ground, still hypnotized. Aubrey spun around and grabbed my arm, throwing me to the ground too. I did not immediately try to stand. I did not want to fight him again, because I knew that if I lost, he would kill me.

"You never learn, do you?" he snapped. "Stand up, Risika."

I stood slowly, watching him warily, but he only pulled Katherine to her feet.

She had caught her hand in a raspberry bush when she fell, and I had to turn my head away from her, my already faltering self-control weakened further by the scent of blood.

104

Once again Aubrey pulled her head back, and this time my gaze caught on her throat, riveted by the blood that was flowing just beneath the surface. I hesitated an instant, during which Aubrey leaned forward. He showed no reluctance as his fangs pierced her throat.

"Let her go, Aubrey," I somehow managed to growl, fighting the bloodlust that was trying to convince me to feed.

He looked up, and his black gaze met mine for a moment; he licked blood from his lips, and a wicked smile spread across his face. "You really want me to?"

"*Yes,*" I snapped back.

"Here."

He pushed the woman into my arms, then disappeared.

I stumbled, shocked, but when I recovered I found myself holding the unconscious woman gently.

Her bleeding hand was resting on my arm, and I could feel her pulse beating against my skin. A thin line of blood ran down her throat, and before I even realized what I was doing, I had licked it away.

I felt every pulse of her heart as if it was my own, and each beat was like fire being forced through my veins. I turned my head away, trying to capture some measure of control, but that simple move brought on a spell of dizziness.

I had not fed in days.

The thirst was so strong, and her blood seemed the sweetest I had ever taken. I let it roll across my tongue, savoring the taste, knowing I should not but unable to stop myself.

I heard a hoarse cry, and my head snapped up. I saw my father. There was no recognition in his gaze.

I dropped Katherine, forcing myself to let her go. I had not yet taken enough to harm her; she would survive.

I disappeared into the night.

CHAPTER 18

NOW

After that night I fed well, never again allowing myself to reach the point where I could lose control. Aubrey had accomplished his goal, as always.

My anger at Aubrey turns into anger at myself. Then as now, he managed to use my emotions against me.

Why do you let him make you so upset? I ask myself. *You know he does it intentionally. Why does it continue to bother you?*

"Coward," I say to myself. "That's all you really are — a coward. You've worn that scar for three hundred years, and you've done nothing. You can't even keep your temper long enough to *think!*"

I realize that despite everything I have said, I have still been clinging to some part of my humanity.

For three hundred years I have avoided

him, refusing to fight. When I was human, I was controlled by my father and my church. Now Aubrey controls me, and I do not fight because I am afraid of the consequences. I might die, but that has never been my real fear. I fear that if I start the fight, it will be proof that I am the monster I have tried for so long to pretend I am not.

Who am I pretending for? Alexander used to be my faith. He clung to his morals even when he thought he might be damned, and I have tried to do the same. Why? Alexander is dead, and no one else cares.

So why bother? Why pretend? I ask myself. *You have not been human for nearly three hundred years; stop acting as if you are.*

What else do you have to lose?

I change out of my black tank top into a gold one that hugs my body and shows a bare line of flesh just above my black jeans. My moods change like shadows in a candle flame, and I am in a playful mood now. I sketch the rune of gambling in the air, remembering it from somewhere in my long past: Perthro, shaped like a glass on its side, for people who are willing to bet everything, win or lose.

I am in a far more destructive, reckless mood than ever. I remember the stories I have been told about Jager — how he flirted shamelessly with the virgin followers of Hestia in the Greek era, danced in a fairy ring at midnight under the full moon, and spiced up a ceremony performed by a few modern-day Wiccans by making the elements called actually appear. I am in that kind of mood. I have nothing left to lose, and I want to change something. Destroy something.

I spin the mirror so that it faces away from me. I know what I will see if I look into its reflective illusion.

I bring myself to a small town in upstate New York that is hidden deep in the woods, beyond the sight of the human world, called New Mayhem. *New* Mayhem — the Mayhem Ather showed me three hundred years ago was nearly leveled by a fire a few years after I was first there.

I have been to New Mayhem several times, but I am the only one in my line who does not sleep within its boundaries. Aubrey has his home inside the walls of New Mayhem, and so I have always made mine elsewhere.

Even with the new hotel suites that house the mortals, the new bars, the new gyms, and the paved streets, New Mayhem is still an invisible town. The bartenders never ask for ID, the hotel doesn't keep records of who comes and goes, and the nightclub is as strange as an ice-skating rink in Hell. No one ever comes, no one is ever there, no one ever leaves — at least, there would be no way to prove it should anyone ever look for receipts, or credit card numbers, or any written record of those who were there.

The heart of New Mayhem is a large building on which is painted a jungle mural. Around the doorway pulses a glowing red light from inside the club. This is where I go, barely even reading the name on the door: *Las Noches*.

The red strobe lamp is the only light inside Las Noches, giving the room a spinning, blood-washed effect. Mist covers the floor. The walls are all glass, mostly mirror, but in places there are eyes painted beneath the glass. The tables are polished black wood and look like satanic mushrooms growing from the mist. Pounding music, bass heavy enough that it makes our bodies vibrate in time with the beat, slams down from a speaker somewhere in the shadowed ceiling.

At the counter, which is also black wood, is a black-haired girl called Rabe, one of

New Mayhem's few inhabitants who are completely human. This early in the night Las Noches has a mixed crowd — more human than vampire, actually — but Rabe works here even when the crowd is completely vampire.

I turn away from Rabe and scan the room for the one person I seek. I find him sitting at a table with a human girl, though they do not appear to be talking. I walk purposefully to the back of the room, and ignoring the human, sit on the table. Chairs? Not for me, thank you.

Aubrey's eyes widen, no doubt wondering when I became so bold. I do not look at the human girl, though I know she has not left the table. She is sitting very still, but I can hear her breath and her heartbeat.

"Risika, why are you sitting on the table?" Aubrey finally asks me.

"Why not?"

"There are chairs," he points out. The girl behind me is slowly standing, inching away as if I might reach out and grab her if she catches my attention. I almost laugh. I am already smiling — the slow, lazy, mischievous smile of a cat.

"It seems your date is leaving, Aubrey," I comment, and the girl freezes. "Is she more afraid of me than she is of you?"

"Go away, Christina," Aubrey says to the frightened girl, who darts off.

"You have no class, Aubrey."

He frowns momentarily at my words but then decides to ignore them. "I forgot to comment on your new style of hair, Risika," he says. "It reminds me of that dumb beast in the zoo."

"I noticed that you tied her up before you killed her. Was one tiger too much for you to handle?"

We play this deadly game well, each of us striking at the other without blows — and it is indeed a deadly game. Who will lose their temper first? Who will strike the first physical blow?

"Risika, no one creature is too much for me to handle," Aubrey laughs.

"Oh, brave Aubrey," I say. "Save us from the defenseless animals!"

He shoves my shoulder, taking me by surprise and pushing me off the table. Then he stands. So far he has not drawn a weapon.

I sit on the floor, in the mist, and laugh. "You fool," I say. "You complete fool."

Chapter 19

NOW

Several of the humans have gathered around us, wondering what is going on. This is not a smart thing to do when two vampires fight. However, humans are curious to the point of stupidity, and they do not think about possible casualties if the fight gets out of hand.

I stand from the mist, my laughter gone from the air but still in both our minds.

"You're like a child, Aubrey," I say. "The neighborhood bully, I suppose. You can terrorize humans and children, but what would happen if someone fought you who knew what they were doing?"

"Get out, Risika. I don't want to fight you again. We've done this before." His voice is cold, meant to frighten, but I do not heed it.

"We've done this before, have we? Where is your fancy blade then, Aubrey? You offered it to me and asked me to kill you if I could. I think I deserve a second chance."

"Why do you feel compelled to challenge me again, Risika? You still wear the scar I gave you last time. Are you so determined to bear another?"

"I wear this scar as a sign that I will one day repay it. 'Do unto others as you would have them do unto you,' Aubrey. I will avenge this scar and every scar you have put into my heart."

"Really? How, Risika?" he asks me, leaning against the table casually. "I am far older than you —"

"Does it matter, Aubrey?" I respond, slowly circling him. He does not turn to keep me in sight until I am completely behind him, but he does turn. He does not like having me at his back.

"Perhaps not, but I am meaner, Risika, and I am deadlier. A viper, hidden in the grass."

A viper — how apt. Does he know how often I have compared him to that exact creature?

"A garden snake, Aubrey, hiding in the grass. I am not weak anymore, but I think you are." I lean forward, my hands on the table between us.

I am lying, of course. I know he is

stronger than I, but I am not about to admit that to him.

"That remains to be seen, does it not?" he answers, turning away from me as if he doesn't care where I am.

Another deadly game. We circle each other. *I am not afraid to have you behind me — I do not fear you that much,* we say to each other. Yet we watch our backs, because we are both vipers, willing to kill and simply waiting for a chance.

"Shall we find out?" I suggest coolly. I am not bothering to hide my aura, and I can feel it stretch out, strike Aubrey's aura, and crackle around it. I search his aura, looking for weaknesses, as I know he searches mine.

"Why are you so eager to lose, Risika?"

He *is* afraid of me, I realize. He is playing for time — trying to make me lose my nerve. Why? Because he is afraid he might lose? It does not seem possible that Aubrey thinks I could win.

I walk around the table toward him until I am close enough that he turns, not trusting me.

"Why are you stalling, Aubrey?" My power snaps out and hits his like a whip. He staggers a bit — I am strong, and I am reckless, and I really do *not* like him.

His own power lashes out, and I feel a burning in my veins. My vision mists over for a moment, a moment in which Aubrey draws his knife.

"You always need your blade, don't you, Aubrey? Because without it you'd lose, wouldn't you?" I circle behind him, and he turns to keep me in sight. Like the game of insults, this is one I can win: Follow me, watch me, but do not let me get behind you, because you know I hate you and will kill you if given a chance. It is only in the actual fight that I fear I might lose.

"Come now, Aubrey — just like old times. You threw your blade down then and dared me to pick it up; are you too afraid to do so now?"

I lash my power around his wrist. His muscles spasm, but he holds on to the knife.

" 'Yea, though I walk through the valley of the shadow of death, I will fear no evil.' I have nothing to fear, Aubrey — what about you?"

His power flares out with his anger, and I hear wood crack. One of the tables splits down the middle, and a human jumps out of the way barely in time.

"Impressive," I say scornfully, and lash out with my own power. The mirrored

116

walls fracture into spiderweb patterns with no single inch left whole. Hairline cracks run through every surface, but not one piece falls out. Aubrey backs up a step, away from me.

"Coward," I say. "Do you back away from me?" I take a step forward, ever aware of the knife in his hand, and he steps back again, almost running into one of the humans, who jumps away quickly.

Aubrey glances behind him and notices the crowd for the first time. It is mostly human, but there are some of our kind. I see Jager lounging against the wall and Fala, Jager's fledgling, sitting cross-legged on a table.

"Are you all talk, Aubrey? Are you too afraid to fight?" I circle to the left as he moves to get behind me, so that I end up behind him. Once again he has to turn to keep me in his sight.

"Why would I be afraid?" he asks, his tone mocking. "It would not hurt me to destroy you, Risika."

"I'm sure it wouldn't, Aubrey, but we will never have a chance to test the theory," I answer.

"Test it again, you mean," he says. "We have tested it once before."

I ignore his words and reach out, my

aura striking his in its center and latching on. The average human sees nothing, and the vampires see only a shimmering space between us, but Aubrey feels it, and I feel it.

He stumbles again, bringing his shields up and throwing my power back at me. I hold on with my mind, though I fall into a table, and feel his power crackling around my own.

Humans have one thing to use in a fight: their bodies. Among my kind, opponents fight with their bodies, but also with their minds. I can feel Aubrey's power beating against my shields, trying to get into my mind, trying to latch on to my own power. I push him away from my mind, trying to get into his, all the while circling, moving closer, dodging the knife, circling away.

My eyes mist over for a moment, and my veins burn as Aubrey lashes out again. I stumble, and he strikes out with his blade. I narrowly dodge, falling back, barely catching myself before I fall to the floor. Aubrey is there in a moment, but I am not.

His power, which has attached itself to my aura, keeps me from using my mind to move. But I push him back long enough to change to hawk form and fly away. Fighting his mind and holding hawk form is nearly impossible, and I return to human form. Aubrey's mind is stronger than my own, but for the first time I realize that the difference is small. Were he as strong as I thought, he could have stopped me from changing at all.

I came here expecting to lose but refusing to run. For the first time I realize I might be able to win.

Aubrey's power wavers for a moment as my fear drops, and I strike out again with all my strength. Aubrey falls back a few feet, and I advance and strike again. He disappears for a moment, and suddenly the knife is at my throat.

I know that if I use the small strength I have left to move, I will not be able to hold up the walls keeping him out of my mind.

Chapter 20

NOW

I freeze, feeling the faintest burning where the blade presses against the skin of my throat. With that blade, it will be fatal if my throat is slit.

"I told you long ago that you cannot win against me, Risika." Aubrey thinks he has won, and he is not paying as much attention to his shields. I do not feel him pushing as strongly against my mind. Why fight when you think you have won? "I do not kill my own unless forced to, Risika, and you are not enough of a threat to force me. So go."

He moves the knife away for a moment, and I hit his wrist, breaking it. The knife falls to the ground, and I shove him into the fractured mirrors that make up the walls.

I laugh.

I pick up the knife before he can recover,

striking him with my mind, keeping his shields down. I lock on to his mind with my own, forcing him down.

"Aubrey, I've learned. In fact, you taught me this little trick. You think that once you turn your back I will stay away, afraid. Well, know this, Aubrey," I say, feeding his words back to him. "That isn't how the world works."

Now he begins to fight again. He was taken by surprise for a moment, but he grows desperate. He lashes out along the line of power I am using to strike him, and as I stumble for a moment, losing my hold, his walls return.

We both now know that this fight is serious. But he is weak, and I can feel that he is afraid. He has forgotten his knife, which I now hold; his every instinct is focused on survival.

I throw his strike back at him, forcing him away from my mind. He stumbles slightly but then throws all his power at me. I fall into the table Fala sits upon and instantly feel her power strike out against me. For just a moment I lose focus, dropping the knife, and Aubrey pins me to the ground.

He has retrieved his knife.

This scene is familiar. I remember three

hundred years ago, lying upon the forest ground, Aubrey pinning me, knife in hand. The memory brings a thread of terror, and I react instinctively. I do what I was not able to do then.

I throw Aubrey off me — not far, just a foot or so. But in the moment when he is off balance I shift into another form I know inside and out, one with the strength to fight.

The Bengal tiger is the largest feline on earth. Aubrey does not know the mind of a tiger, the pure animal instinct, and cannot find a hold. I slash at him, scoring his chest. The wounds heal in moments, but I have pushed him down again.

Aubrey tries to roll away, but I pin him to the ground. I am physically stronger than Aubrey, and though he is stronger when using his mind to fight, my mind is powerful enough to hold him off when I am in this form.

I look into his eyes, in which I can see a flicker of fear beneath a sheet of resignation. He almost looks as if he was expecting this moment.

I prepare for a killing strike. But he does not want to die.

"You've proved yourself, Risika," he tells me. "Years ago I gave you a choice between giving up and fighting to the death. Do I get no such chance?"

I hesitate. *Aubrey, I know how this game works,* I answer with my mind, as I cannot speak the human tongue when I am in this form. *If I let you go now, what is to stop you from stabbing me in the back as soon as I turn away?*

This doesn't need to be to the death, Risika, Aubrey insists. I can sense his desperation.

You gave me a choice because I was weak, Aubrey. I am stronger than you — we have proved that here — but I swore long ago that I would avenge all you have taken from me. And you took so much; the price is so high.

He moves his head back, exposing his throat, and I pause, waiting for him to explain. *I paid a high price long ago for this life. I do not want it to end yet,* he tells me with his mind. *I offer you my blood in return for the blood I have spilled.*

He is serious. The fool really would do anything to survive. My taking his blood would make me far stronger and open his mind to me completely. There would be no way for him to shield his mind from me, and no way for him to harm me with his mind, which would make it nearly impossible for him to hurt me. Physically he would have the same strength, but he

123

could make no move that I could not read from his mind ahead of time.

I pause for only a moment, then return to human form and lean forward. My teeth pierce skin, and the blood flows. Vampire blood is far stronger than human blood.

His blood tastes like white wine, only thicker and far more potent, and I feel giddy when I pull away again, wiping blood from my lips. The wound on his throat heals instantly, but I know the wound to his pride will last as long as I do.

I pick Aubrey's knife up off the ground and contemplate it for a moment. He is defenseless, and if I struck him in the heart he could not raise a hand to protect himself. I trace the scar from my throat to my shoulder, remembering, and then, like lightning, I draw the knife along Aubrey's collarbone in an identical wound.

"Remember this day, Aubrey. The wound you dealt long ago has returned to you. I'll be satisfied with your blood, though it doesn't begin to replace the lives of Alexander and Tora. Now get out."

I let go of his mind, yet I can still feel it completely. It is an eerie sensation. I stand easily, his blood racing through my veins, replacing the power I lost in the fight and far more.

Aubrey pulls himself up into a sitting position, using a nearby table. His skin is flour white, and his eyes are almost empty as he raises his hand to the wound on his shoulder. No one has ever wounded him and lived to tell of it.

He slowly stands to leave, and the humans move away as he walks through them. Those that remain know what we are, and they know what such blood loss has done to his hunger and how hard it is for him to maintain his control as he leaves the room.

I turn my back on him, unafraid, and return my gaze to Fala, who is still sitting serenely on the table. She does not seem to remember almost causing my death.

I lash out with my power, and she jumps up gracelessly as the wooden table catches fire. Fala disappears, not wanting to fight.

CHAPTER 21

NOW

I walk toward Jager, and humans bump into each other to get out of my way. I laugh as they hurry from the room.

"Come to see the show?" I ask him.

"I told you you were stronger than Aubrey," he says. "The coward. I didn't expect him to offer so much just to live. You are probably one of the strongest of us now — maybe as strong as I. It would be interesting to find out."

"Another time, Jager," I answer. The adrenaline and energy from the fight are still in me, and part of me wants to fight something stronger. But the rational part of my mind tells me I am far too giddy to fight anyone seriously.

"Of course, Risika," he agrees. Jager fights simply for the challenge, not for a prize, and he does not fight anyone who he does not think has a fair chance unless it is necessary. At the moment I am drunk on Aubrey's blood, and I would lose. "Your eyes are still golden from shifting to a tiger," he tells me.

"I like them this way." I laugh, looking into the shattered mirror. My once misty reflection is now completely gone, but I can see myself in my mind's eye. My hair is still tiger striped, and my eyes are as golden as my silk tank top — the color they were when I was alive, before vampirism darkened them to black. I run my tongue along my teeth, licking off the last traces of Aubrey's blood.

Jager disappears, and I realize that almost everyone has left. Tossing a black strand of hair off my face, I feel for the first time a familiar aura in the back of the room. I remember it from a letter I received recently, a letter with a tearstain on the page.

"So my stalker would visit me in person," I say to his back. In this light the blond hair looks almost exactly as my own once did. I reach out with my mind, and even though I cannot read him I realize what he is. I remember the Triste witch who had been in the Café Sangra, who had given a note for Rachel to his vampiric victim.

I did not think much about it at the moment, but now I wish I had. I swear, suddenly realizing the truth I should have realized long ago.

"I was hoping I could convince you not to follow those creatures . . . but I guess it's too late, isn't it?"

I remember wondering why I never heard him fall.

"Rachel —" he starts to say.

"Alexander, don't talk to me." He has waited three hundred years to tell me he is alive? I damned myself years ago. I had — or thought I had — nothing left to lose, then. All the years I was alone. All the pain he could have spared me . . .

What pain has he known? I never went back to my father, because I did not want him to see what I had become. Had I known my twin was alive, and immortal like me, would I have chosen to spend the years with him? Would he choose to spend them with me, knowing I'm a monster?

He turns around, and for a moment I look into golden eyes that are mirror reflections of my own. But then he looks past me, at the area where Aubrey and I fought. I see Alexander's gaze linger on the blood that pooled on the ground when I cut open Aubrey's shoulder.

"Why?" he finally asks, his voice soft. "There had to be some other way to deal with this."

I look into Alexander's eyes again and see the judgment there. It does not matter that I am his sister. He *does* think I am a monster.

I laugh, and Alexander flinches, because it is a bitter sound. "Would you rather I just let Aubrey get away with it?" I say. "I thought he killed you, you know. Did you want me to just *forget* that? Or did you think I could turn the other cheek and ignore murder?" Alexander looks away for a moment, pain filling his features as he hears my scornful use of words from the Bible, which he always held so dear when we were children.

"I thought you would hate me for what I had done," he says.

"And just what have you done?"

He pauses, shaking his head, and then reluctantly meets my gaze. "After Lynette was burnt, I would have done anything to protect her. I prayed that I would learn how to control my power, and . . ." He takes a deep breath, steadying himself. "A woman heard me praying. A Triste. She taught me more than I ever wanted to know about the vampires and every other monster on this Earth. I listened because she also taught me how to use my gifts."

From a curse to a gift, I think. *Does he still consider himself damned?*

"A few nights before Ather . . . changed you . . . I caught her trying to feed off Lynette. I stopped her, but . . ."

I can guess the rest of the story. Ather is too proud to let anyone take away her prey without seeking revenge. She changed me to hurt Alexander, because my faithful brother would be torn apart by his sister's damnation.

Alexander pulls his gaze from mine, and this time it falls to Aubrey's blood on my hands. "Rachel, how could you do that? I never thought I'd see you with blood on you, willing to kill another. You walk with them as if you are one of them."

I could argue — after all, I did not kill Aubrey — but I do not.

I loved Alexander long ago, and I suppose I still do. But things have changed in three hundred years. At least, I have changed. Alexander does not understand.

He tried to protect me once. He tried to keep me away from the darkness and death, because he did not want Ather to change me into what I now am. He tried, but he did not succeed, and there is no way to undo the damage that has been done since. I have been a monster too long, and as much as I care about him, I cannot change my nature now.

My golden brother still does not belong in this dark world. His sister is dead, long dead, and I cannot bring her back to protect him from all the pain I know seeing me has given him.

The only way I can protect him now is to make sure he never understands how easy killing can become.

"Alexander, listen closely. Rachel is dead," I say, forcing my voice to be cold so that he will not argue. I speak quietly, driving my words to his brain. "I am one of them."

I consider the words as I say them. It is true — I *am* one of them. But no one — not Aubrey, not Ather, not my father or brother — controls me now.

I could have killed Aubrey. I could have used my strength to be like him. But I remember my humanity.

I am one of them.

But I am also Rachel.

I am Risika.

About the Author

AMELIA ATWATER-RHODES is fourteen years old and lives in Concord, Massachusetts. She wrote *In the Forests of the Night* when she was thirteen. *In the Forests of the Night* is her first novel.